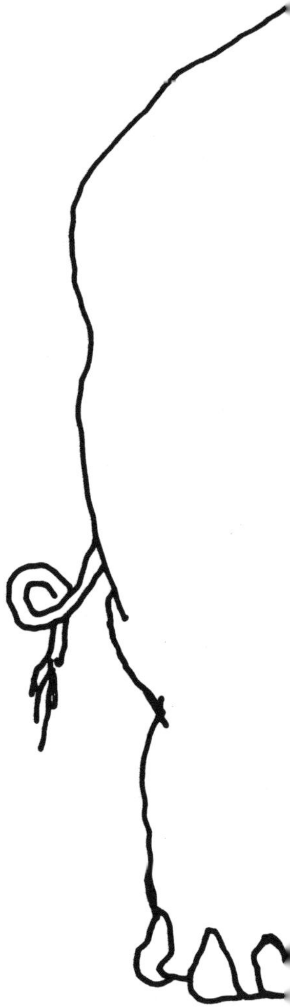

Who

wants a cheap Rhinoceros?

by Shel Silverstein

SIMON & SCHUSTER BOOKS FOR YOUNG READERS
New York London Toronto Sydney Singapore

Revised and expanded edition of a book previously published
under the pseudonym, Uncle Shelby

SIMON & SCHUSTER BOOKS FOR YOUNG READERS
An imprint of Simon & Schuster Children's Publishing Division
1230 Avenue of the Americas
New York, New York 10020

Book design by Kim Llewellyn
The text of this book is set in Bembo.
The illustrations are rendered in pen and ink.
Printed in China
10 9 8 7 6 5

Library of Congress Cataloging-in-Publication Data
Silverstein, Shel. Rev. and expanded ed.
Who wants a cheap rhinoceros?
Summary: There are lots of things a rhino can do around one's house, including eating bad report cards before one's parents see them, tiptoeing downstairs for a midnight snack, and collecting extra allowance.
1. Rhinoceros—Fiction. I. Title.
PZ7.S588Wh 2002 [E] 2002070578

ISBN 0-689-85113-8

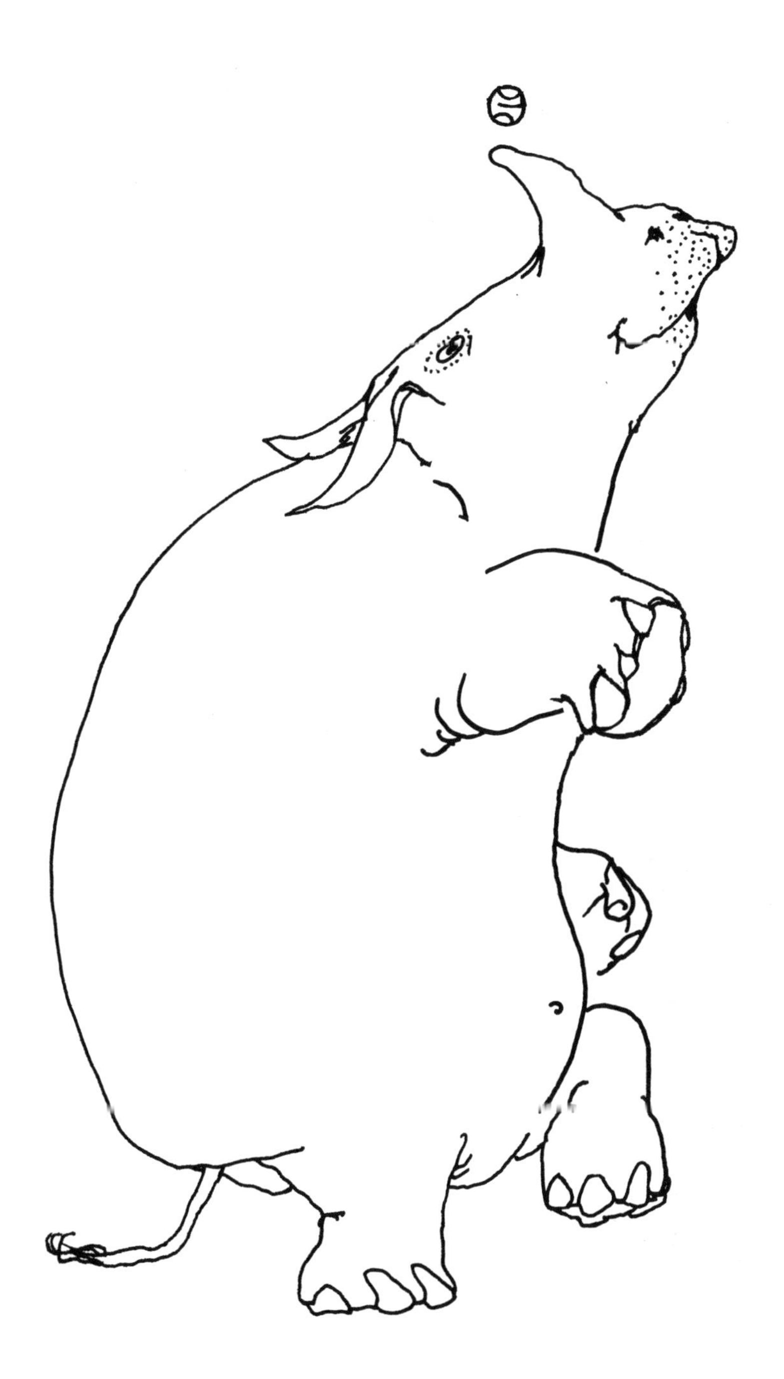

To Meg and Curt

Who wants a cheap rhinoceros?
I know of one for sale,
With floppy ears and cloppy feet,
And friendly waggy tail.
He's sweet and fat and huggable.
He's quiet as a mouse.
And there are lots of things that he
Can do around your house.

For instance. . .

You can use him for a coat hanger.

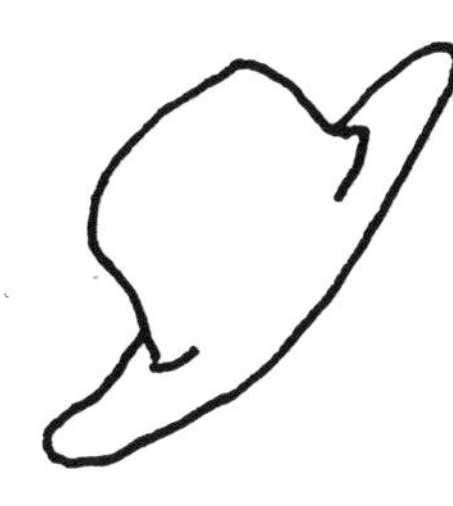

He is a terrific back scratcher.

And he makes a very lovely lamp.

He will eat bad report cards
before your parents see them.

But he is not too great at opening doors.

He makes a good bloody ferocious pirate.

He can open soda cans for your uncle.

And on Sunday
you can read him
the comics.

He will be glad to turn a jump rope...

. . . if he gets his turn.

He’s not too careful about
watching where he walks.

But he's very handy for collecting
extra allowance from your father.

He makes an unsinkable battleship.

But he is not too interested in taking his bath.

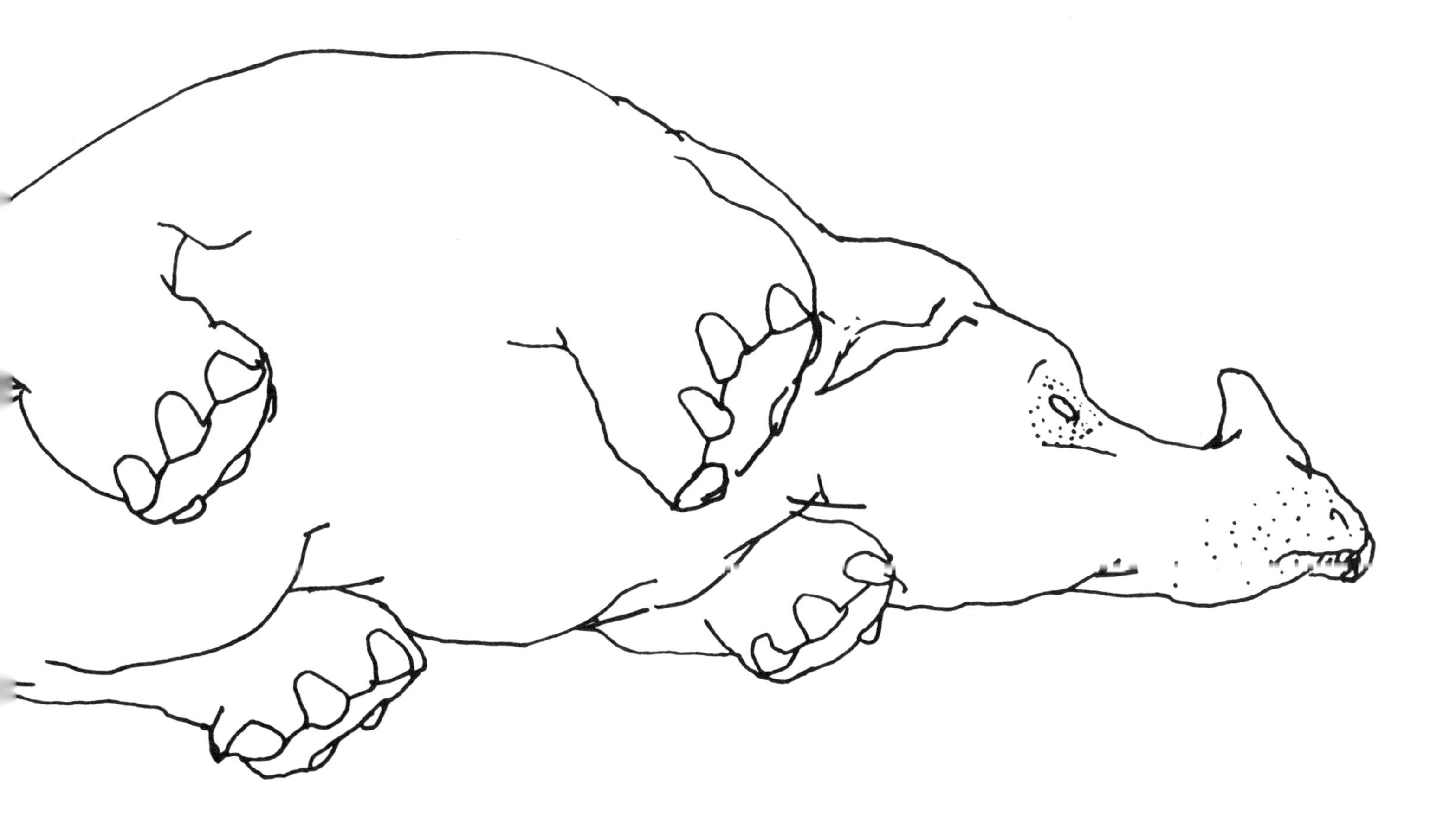

It is
very
comfortable
when
you sit
on his
lap.

but
not too
comfortable
when
he sits
on your
lap.

He's terrific at helping
your grandmother make donuts.

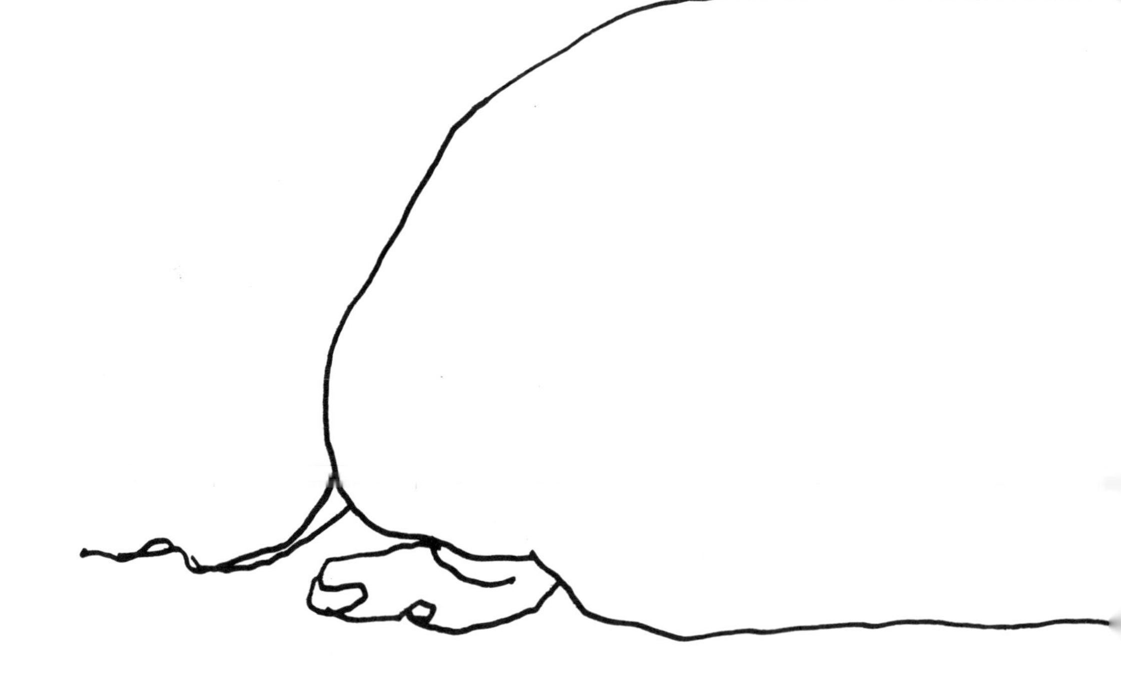

And he is great for not letting your mother hit you
when you haven't really done anything bad.

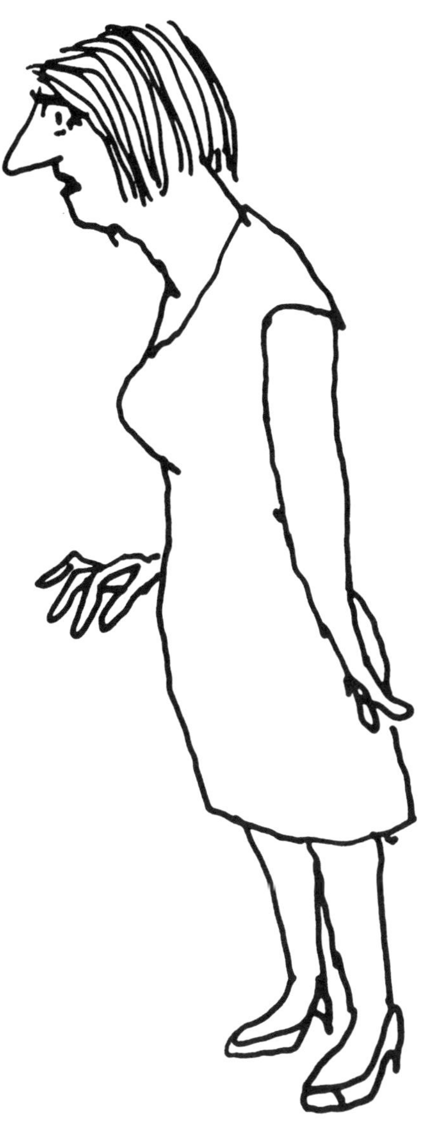

He is very nice about crawling into bed
with you on cold winter nights,

and he is pretty good at
tiptoeing downstairs
for a midnight
snack.

And he'll gladly eat scraps from the table.

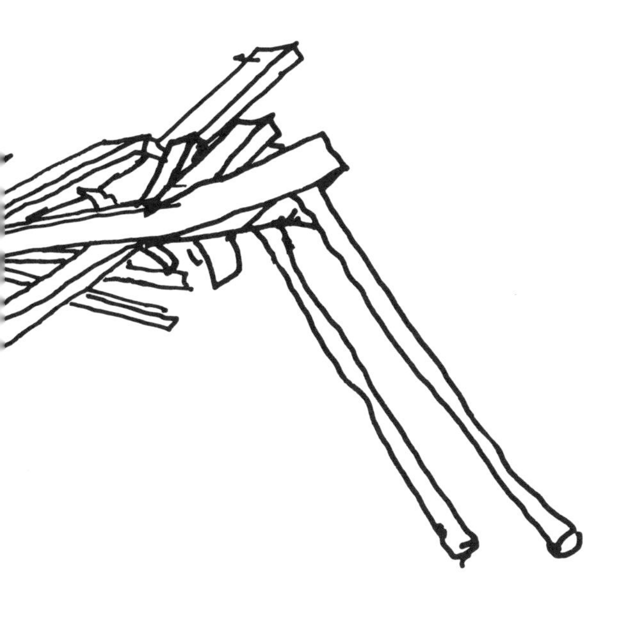

He is terrific at being Ben and Charlie,
two desperate crooks.

And he loves to surprise you.

He will be glad to help your aunt knit a sweater.

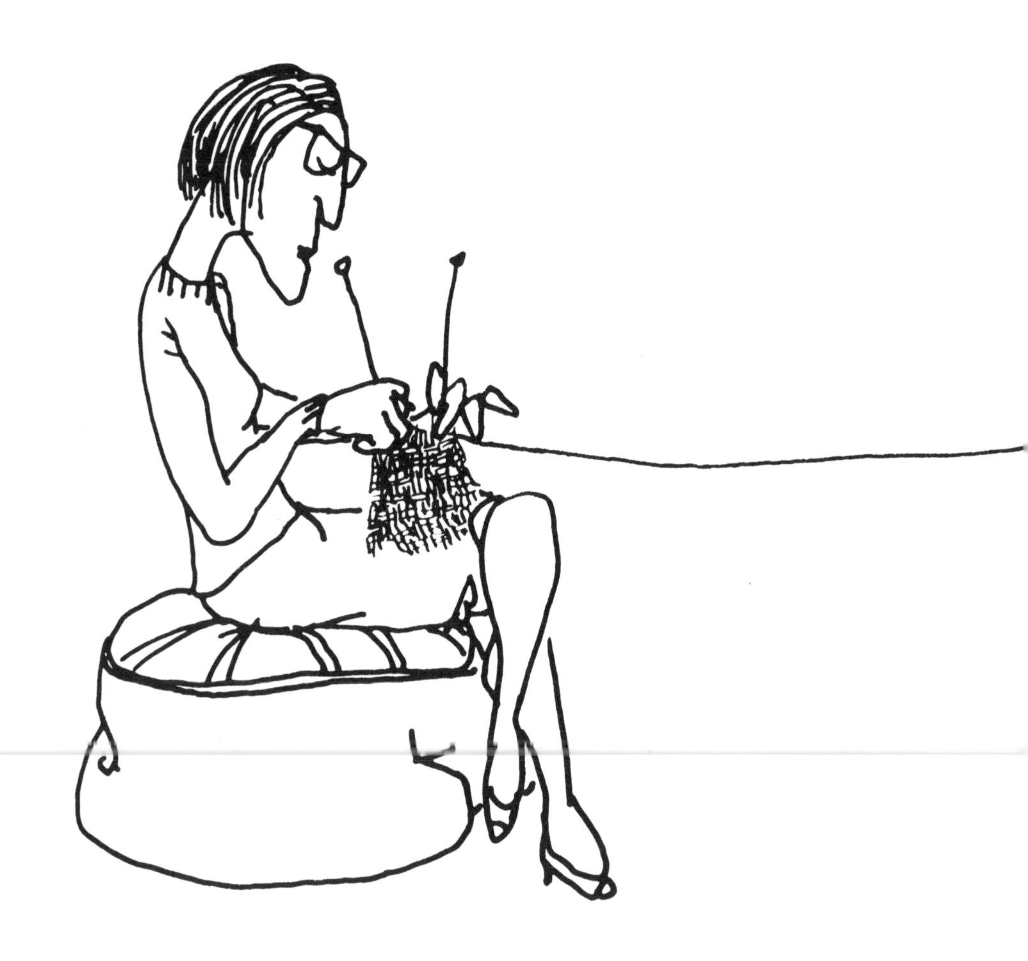

Especially if it is for him.

He is careful about not leaving rhinoceros
tracks around the house.

He is fun to take care of
when he is sick.

And he is great for
plowing your field
if you are a
farmer.

He is hard
to build a
house for.

But he is lots of fun
at the beach

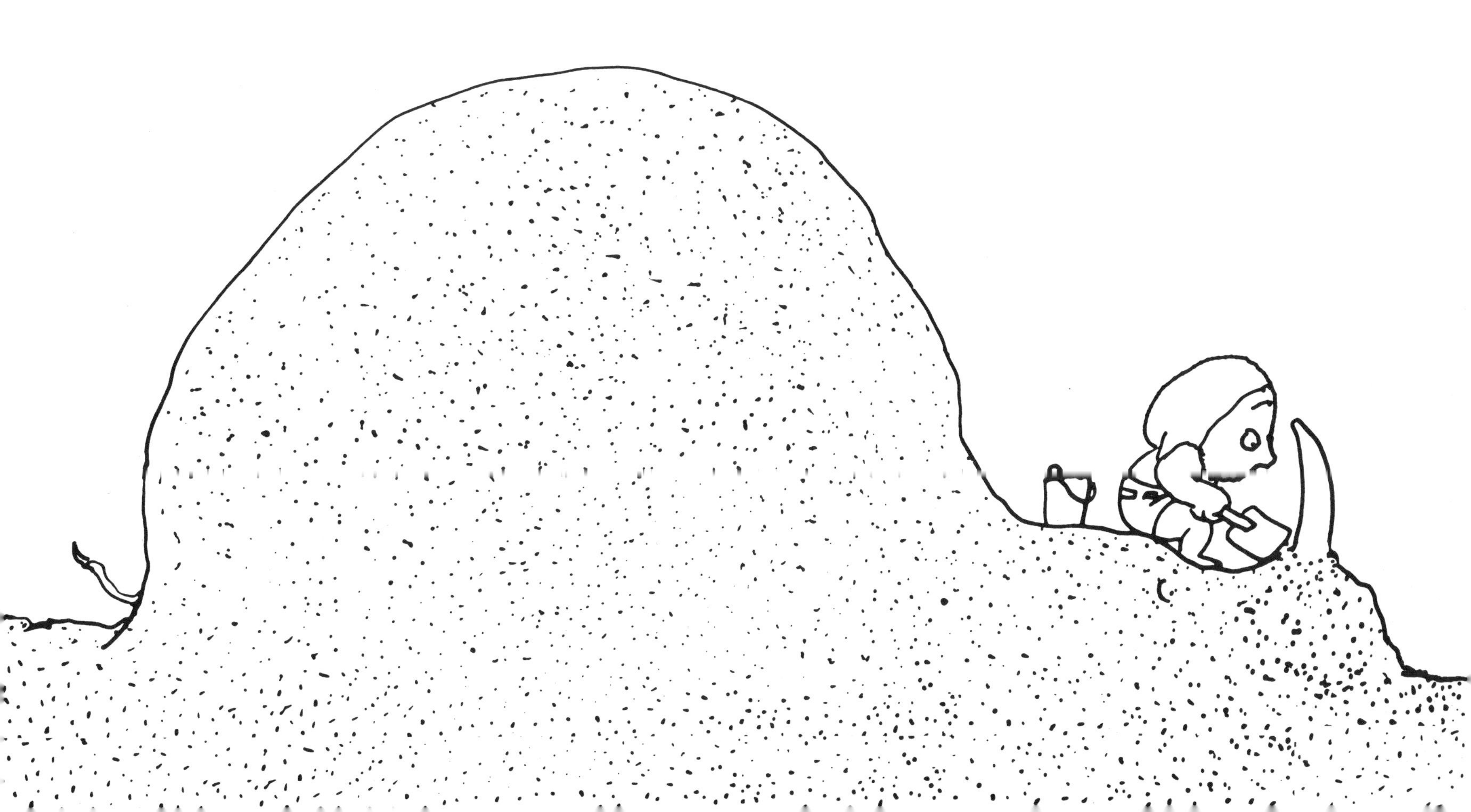

because he is great at imitating a shark.

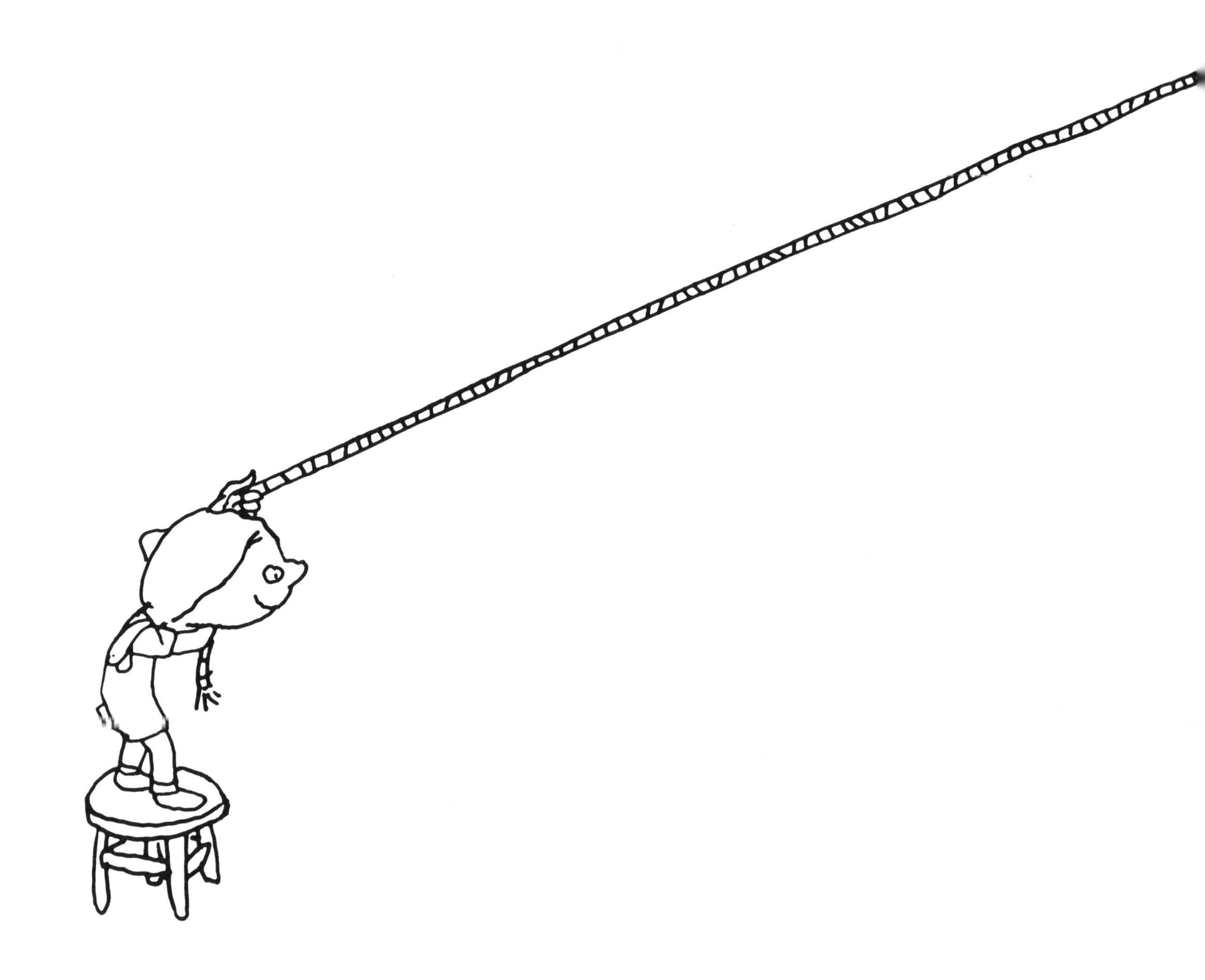

He is wonderful
for playing records
if you have
no record player.

And on Halloween you can dress him up like a girl—but he won't like it.

He loves to play
hide and seek.

He is good for yelling at.

And he is easy to love.